I0633620

The World Outside My Window

Ruskin Bond has been writing for over sixty years, and now has over 120 titles in print—novels, collections of short stories, poetry, essays, anthologies and books for children. His first novel, *The Room on the Roof*, received the prestigious John Llewellyn Rhys Award in 1957. He has also received the Padma Shri (1999), the Padma Bhushan (2014) and two awards from Sahitya Akademi— one for his short stories and another for his writings for children. In 2012, the Delhi government gave him its Lifetime Achievement Award.

Born in 1934, Ruskin Bond grew up in Jamnagar, Shimla, New Delhi and Dehradun. Apart from three years in the UK, he has spent all his life in India, and now lives in Mussoorie with his adopted family.

RUSKIN
BOND

The World Outside My Window

RUPA

Published by
Rupa Publications India Pvt. Ltd 2016
7/16, Ansari Road, Daryaganj
New Delhi 110002

Sales Centres:

Allahabad Bengaluru Chennai
Hyderabad Jaipur Kathmandu
Kolkata Mumbai

ISBN: 978-81-291-4179-8

First impression 2016

10 9 8 7 6 5 4 3 2 1

The moral right of the author has been asserted.

Contents

Birdsong in the Mountains

The Loveliness of Ferns

The Wonderful World of Insects

The Wonderful World of Insects

When you have some time to spare, make a list of all the different insects that you can name. If you can put more than twenty names on your list, you will probably do better than the average person. But suppose you knew the name of every kind of insect in India or even in the world. If you were to write them all down, it would take you at least a month, without stopping to sleep or eat, to complete your list. There are over a million species, with thousands more being discovered each year.

When you have made your list, look it over carefully, for it is quite possible that you have included some animals that are not insects at all. Scorpions, spiders and mites are often mistaken for insects, but—though I have included them in this book—they belong to another group of small animals. If you know what to look for, it is quite easy to tell whether or not an animal is an insect.

A moth, a honeybee and a mosquito do not look very much alike, yet each is an insect. If you examine them, you will find certain similarities. Each one of these animals has six legs, as all insects have, with a body divided into three parts: a head, a centre part, and an abdomen. If you remember these two characteristics, you will be able to recognize an insect. The next time you look at a spider, you will see that it has not six but eight legs, and its body only two parts instead of three. For this reason it is not called an insect.

The skeleton of an insect is external, and the muscles and nerves inside are not only protected by this outer covering but combine with it to make the creature surprisingly strong and durable. For example, a beetle can support, without collapsing, some eight hundred times its own weight!

Insects are found almost everywhere—from steaming jungles to polar regions, in the soil, in the air and in the water. They seem to be able to live and thrive under almost any conditions. They have no lungs but breathe through air ducts in the sides of the body, the air being circulated to all parts through an intricate system of tiny tubes.

In beauty and colour some insects have no equal in the animal world, while structurally each one is a miracle.

The compound eyes of an insect are composed of many units or separate eyes, each of which transmits an image of what is seen to the brain. They enable the insect to detect the slightest movement of its enemy or prey.

The number of eye-units vary with different insects. The silver fish has 12, some ants have 50, cockroaches 1,800, houseflies 4,000, butterflies 17,000 and dragonflies from 20,000 to 30,000. In addition to the compound eyes, most insects have simple eyes—usually three placed on top of the forehead—which only distinguish between light and dark. Some beetles have two simple eyes placed on the back of the head.

The energy of an insect is tremendous. A flea can jump over one hundred times its height. A mosquito in flight has a wing-beat of three hundred per second. A dragonfly can attain a speed of nearly sixty miles an hour. The Painted Lady butterfly makes a migratory trip from North Africa to as far as Iceland.

Anyone who has stepped on a cockroach, been bitten by a mosquito or bothered by flies, will tell you that some insects are a nuisance. They not only interfere with our activities at times, but they also do damage to the extent of crores of rupees each year in our country alone. Most of the damage is done by insects that feed on plants that we use, insects such as the cotton-destroying boll weevil, the potato beetle and the tobacco hornworm. Also, some kinds of insects—especially flies—carry diseases, and we try to control them on this account.

But not all insects are harmful.

If all insects were to suddenly disappear from the earth, it would not be long before many other living things would vanish too, possibly even mankind.

Many vegetables and flowering plants would die, for these

plants cannot bear fruit or seeds unless an insect transfers their pollen. Fishes and birds that feed on insects would vanish, and many of the animals that depend, in turn, on these fishes and birds for food would soon starve.

Once a link in nature's chain of life is broken or removed, the entire chain is in danger of falling apart.

The Life of the Butterfly

If we catch a female butterfly and keep it in a suitable cage, it will lay eggs. The eggs are small white seed-like things, laid singly on the leaves of a plant. If we keep these eggs, they will presently hatch into caterpillars. These are somewhat worm-like in appearance, with legs and sucker-feet; they are totally different from butterflies in habits and structure.

Caterpillars eat the leaves of plants, and moult (shed their skin) as they grow larger. At each moult the colour changes very slightly and the caterpillar comes out much larger. There are five such moults, and at the end of twelve or fifteen days the caterpillar attains its full size. It now ceases to feed, becomes uneasy; it is preparing for another, different moult.

The caterpillar fastens a small pad of silk at some point on the leaf of the plant, and fixing the hooks of its tail-feet in the silk, hangs itself head downwards from the pad. The skin bursts and is thrown off and the insect is seen hanging from the leaf. It is now completely changed in appearance and is called a chrysalis—a rounded green object, with pretty gold markings. There are no limbs, no mouth, no eyes. This curious creature hangs motionless from the plant for six days, taking no food and appearing to be asleep.

At the end of six days, the outer skin again bursts and a large insect comes out. This walks feebly about for a few minutes whilst its large wings expand and spread out. These wings become firm and stiff, and we see that it is the butterfly again, similar to the one we first caught. This butterfly will fly away, mate and lay eggs, which will again hatch into caterpillars.

Similar changes take place in the life of every butterfly. We see it in four stages—the egg, the caterpillar, the chrysalis and the butterfly.

Caterpillars have many enemies, and only a small percentage survive to turn into butterflies. Birds eat them. So do ants. And every tree swarms with spiders, not web spiders but wolf spiders, which run about in quest of their prey. Then come wasps and ichneumon flies, and these, from the caterpillar's point of view, are of two sorts—those that will carry him to their own quarters as food for their children, and those that leave their children with the caterpillar for the purpose of free board and lodging.

The ichneumon fly waits till its victim is sleeping, and then, in one moment, its work is done. It has laid its eggs on or in the body of the caterpillar, and the larva which hatches nourishes itself at the expense of its host. The caterpillar continues to live and feed, moulting as usual; the parasite meanwhile becomes larger and finally causes the death of its host. A caterpillar may contain one or many parasites. As many as seventy small ichneumons have been reared from the body of a cotton stem-boring caterpillar.

Thus we see that the ichneumon fly is a beneficial insect to man, since it is a natural check upon the increase of destructive caterpillars that attack growing crops. There is a different caterpillar for nearly every kind of edible plant—anar, brinjal, castor, cotton, ginger, jute, lemon, maize, pumpkin, til, tobacco and many others—and if caterpillars were able to breed continuously, without any natural checks, they would overrun the earth and devour all vegetable matter. So we see that when one class of insect lives at the expense of another, the direct beneficiary is man. Butterflies, for all their beauty, are not our friends. But the unattractive ichneumon flies are the farmer's allies. Not only do they destroy caterpillars, but also the grubs of beetles and the maggots of flies.

Butterfly Time

April showers
Bring swarms of butterflies
Streaming across the valley
Seeking sweet nectar.
Yellow, gold and burning bright,
Red and blue and banded white.
To my eyes they bring delight!
Theirs a long and arduous flight,
Here today and off tomorrow,
Floating on, bright butterflies,
To distant bowers.
For nature does things in good order:
And birds and butterflies recognize
No man-made border.

The Colour of Insects

The colour of an insect is important to its welfare. Though large numbers of insects have similar colour schemes, no two species have precisely the same form and colour.

The stick insects are so formed as to closely resemble their surroundings and so escape notice. Leaf insects are coloured like leaves, and may be green or dry. Many moths sit with expanded wings and their colour scheme blends so well with the bark on which they sit that they often escape notice. Grasshoppers, too, have protective colouring, some being of a dry-grass colour and others a green-grass colour. Grasshoppers that live in the fields have roughened backs, like lumps of soil.

An insect sometimes undergoes a change in its colour scheme when surroundings make this necessary. Thus, a young grasshopper that lives in green grass is green, but changes to the colour of dry-grass when the grass ripens and the insect becomes full grown. A caterpillar that sits on a leafy tree is green; but when it has to crawl down the trunk to reach the ground and pupate (change into an adult), it becomes brown, as the green would make it conspicuous against the bark of the tree. The changes may be very small or they may be very marked, and bear a close relation to the differing habits of the young and the old insect. Colour changes at each moult, or change of form, helping the insect to adapt to every change of surroundings.

On the other hand, we find some insects very vividly and brightly coloured, and these stand out clearly against their surroundings. These insects are usually distasteful to birds and predaceous insects, because of their taste, odour or the oils they excrete. Their colour scheme is protective inasmuch as it warns all enemies that they are unpleasant to eat! A young insect-eating bird will remember an unappetizing insect by its vivid colours, and will leave it alone at the next encounter.

There are many insects supposed to be warningly coloured: red, orange or yellow with black are common warning colours. Most bees and wasps, ladybird beetles, some blister beetles and some butterflies are so coloured. Dragonflies are often brilliant, with red, blue, yellow, green and other vivid colours combining with black. In fact, some insects, which are tasty, have copied the warning colours of the unpleasant insects, and so managed to survive! This is known as insect mimicry. Edible butterflies mimic nasty ones; moths mimic butterflies; flies mimic moths, bees or wasps.

It must not be thought that an insect can change its colour

by itself. The colour of insects is fixed, and all of a species are coloured much alike; but it is believed that during the evolution of insects, they 'adopted' or gradually acquired different colour schemes, and that the warning-coloured insects arose first and the others later.

The leaf butterfly is an interesting example of deceptive colouring. The upper wings are brightly coloured. When it suddenly settles with wings folded, it exactly resembles a dead leaf. Even the grasshopper's lower wings are often brilliant, but, when it settles with folded wings, its colours blend perfectly with the dry grass, making it extremely difficult for a bird to spot it.

Many butterflies have beautiful colouring, which does not fall into any of the above schemes. Some have distinctive marks on the tips of their wings. These are supposed to mislead any bird that attempts to seize them, the bird snatching at the bright spot on the wing and so missing the butterfly, which may lose a part of its wing but still escape alive.

A few insects have a colour scheme that is meant to terrify an enemy or frighten it away. Such are the hawk-moth caterpillars, which when alarmed suddenly expose large eye-like spots and look like ferocious snakes. Many caterpillars have such devices, coloured spots and stripes and waving hair tassels.

Self-preservation is not the only significant reason for an insect's colour. Colours may also help in courtship and mating, as they do in the case of the higher animals, including man. Even from our own point of view, an insect gains in beauty from its colour. So why not from an insect's point of view?

The Dragonfly

A bright, shimmering dragonfly is a beautiful thing, as it goes flitting over the water in summer sunshine, or sits motionless upon a twig with its wings extended and its great eyes gleaming like gold. But not all dragonflies are found near water; some prefer high, dry fields and others like the forest.

dragonflies were so named because of their large appetites and because they eat only living insects, which they pursue through the air. They capture their prey on the wing and feed upon almost all flying insects, especially gnats and mosquitoes. The larger dragonflies eat house flies, wasps and large butterflies.

Many dragonflies are superb fliers and can exceed even birds like swallows in speed and agility. They can alter the direction of their flight with perfect ease, and they seldom fail to capture their prey. Most of this insect's life is spent on the wing. Because the legs are bunched far forward, they are unsuited for walking, and a dragonfly uses them only for clinging and climbing; but once on the wing, the dragonfly can attain a speed of nearly sixty miles an hour.

Like many birds and butterflies, some dragonflies migrate to warmer lands in the autumn, and great swarms have frequently been seen many miles out at sea.

dragonflies possess five eyes. Three are simple, and two are compound. The compound eyes are groups of tiny lenses. There are as many as 28,000 lenses in one eye, enabling the dragonfly to see farther and more clearly than most other insects. The upper lenses in the compound eye are larger and are probably used for flying in dim light or at dusk; the lower lenses are smaller and are probably used for flying in the daytime.

The mother dragonfly lays her eggs directly in the water or fastens them to water plants. The eggs hatch into 'nymphs' (baby dragonflies), which immediately swim off in search of something to eat. Dragonfly nymphs are the ogres of ponds and streams, for they will attack creatures twice their own size. Their jaws and legs are very strong. The nymph catches its prey by extending its lower lip forward; when it is not feeding, the long jaw folds up in front of its face. The dragonfly nymph is not particular about its food and will readily devour members of its own family.

The nymph usually moves by crawling, but it can swim by a curious method. Through the centre of the body runs a tube that ends in five tightly fitting valves. When the insect wants to swim, it fills the tube with water and then squirts out the contents forcibly. Thus jet-propelled, the whole body is sent shooting forward.

Nymphs grow by shedding their skin. They may have as many as seven new coats. When they mature, they crawl up water plants, shed their skin and emerge as flying adults.

dragonflies are harmless to man. They are, in fact, of real value, because the nymphs eat mosquito wrigglers in the water and the adults catch the mosquitoes they find hovering over the water.

The Firefly

There was a time when many people in different parts of the world worked or studied by the fitful glow of a luminous insect—the firefly, or 'jugnu' as we call it in India. In China and Japan, for example, needy students often used to read right through the night by firefly light. It must have been a great strain on their eyes, for although the firefly's glow appears brilliant to the human eye, its candle-power (the unit of light measurement) is extremely low. In fact, one scientist has estimated that it would take nearly forty fireflies to equal the illumination given off by a single candle. And yet, this little insect's light-producing mechanism is more efficient than anything we have invented for the purpose, for the simple reason that practically no heat is generated, whereas in our artificial lighting methods there is always some wastage.

But how does the firefly make its light?

In the insect's body there is a substance called luciferin upon which an enzyme (an organic catalyst) reacts, releasing energy in the form of light. There is nothing very strange about this. A rather similar thing happens when we eat: our enzymes react with the food, but in our case they release energy in the form of bodily heat and movement.

Why do these insects need to give off light at all? The answer seems to be that in the darkness of tropical forests where most fireflies live, male and female fireflies are able to signal to each other from considerable distances, the two sexes each having well-defined flash sequences.

In Japan, even today there are insect-dealers who breed and sell fireflies. Kept in large numbers in little gauze-covered cages, they form quaint and beautiful illuminations at parties and festivals. In many parts of Central and South America too, these little insects found use as primitive lanterns and ornaments. Early travellers to the West Indies relate how they saw black people working in their huts by the light of fireflies in perforated gourd lanterns.

But perhaps the strangest story of all man's uses of fireflies as natural lights comes from Java. It is in a kind of pocket light, consisting of a shallow wooden dish with a lid pivoted at one end. At the bottom of the dish is a layer of wax in which the fireflies are stuck. Extra 'bulbs'—fireflies, of course—are kept in a cane tube. But the really unusual thing about this torch is that it is said to have been used by a burglar. It would probably have been very useful in such a profession, because the moveable lid could be closed over the fireflies when the light was not needed.

It is perhaps worth mentioning that fireflies are not really flies at all; they are beetles. The glow-worm is also a beetle—though the female is more like a worm than her mate. In comparison with fireflies, glow-worms give off a very feeble glimmer.

Like all beetles, and insects generally, fireflies and glow-worms pass through several distinct stages in their lives. First we have the eggs or ova; next, these hatch as larvae or grubs; then these turn into pupae, which is the final resting stage before the adult firefly emerges to find a mate and begin the whole sequence again.

Most of the firefly's feeding is done by the larvae, as by the larvae (or caterpillars) of butterflies and moths. Some firefly larvae feed on animal matter, others on vegetable. The glow-worm larva, for example, likes nothing better than a meal of slugs and snails; so it deserves all the protection it can get, especially from gardeners.

Firefly in My Room

Last night, as I lay sleepless
In the summer dark
With window open to invite a breeze,
Softly a firefly flew in
And circled round the room
Twinkling at me from floor or wall
Or ceiling, never long in one place
But lighting up little spaces…
A friendly presence, dispelling
The settled gloom of an unhappy day.

And after it had gone, I left
The window open, just in case
It should return.

The Ladybird Beetle

The ladybird beetle is familiar to almost everyone. Like a tiny, brightly coloured minicar, the little insect moves busily over leaves and grass blades, searching for food. Sometimes it turns up in surprising places; on the counterpane of one's bed, or on the curtains or the inside of a windowpane.

Ladybirds, like pills, come in assorted shapes, sizes and colours. Some are oval and some are round. Some are black with red spots and some red with black spots. All of them, however, have six short legs that carry them about with surprising speed, and a pair of dark wings. The wings are kept hidden beneath the two spotted wing-covers and are not usually visible when the ladybird is not using them.

During spring the female ladybird beetle lays her eggs. They are not laid in a group like the eggs of many other insects, but each one is placed on the leaf of a plant. When the egg hatches, out crawls an insect that does not have any resemblance to the adult beetle. It is long and soft, and its legs look almost useless. However, these legs serve the larva, or young grub, in hanging on to a stem or twig. As soon as the larva hatches, it goes in search of food, eating mostly aphids and scale-insects that are very injurious to our plants. Like many other immature insects, the larva outgrows its skin and has to shed it. After several moults, it is ready to change into a pupa. In some secluded spot, it hangs upside down by its tail and sheds its skin for the last time; then the pupa appears with the old skin draped around the top. After a few days, the pupa skin splits and the full-grown ladybird emerges.

The ladybird beetle is an insect that is very helpful to man, for both adult and larva eat some of the most harmful insects. Several years ago, the orange and lemon trees in Californian orchards were being ruined by a species of scale-insect. A new species of Australian ladybird beetle was introduced into California, and within a few years these ladybirds had destroyed the insect pests.

Although the ladybird does not have many enemies, it protects itself quite successfully. If you touch one as it is running along the stem of a plant, it will probably fold its legs underneath its body, drop to the ground and lie as if dead for several minutes. Then, when it thinks the danger has passed, it will suddenly begin waving its legs frantically in an effort to right itself.

Some will remember the nursery rhyme:
'Ladybird, ladybird, fly away home,
Your house is on fire, your children will burn.'

There is not much truth to this, because the ladybird has no house and absolutely no interest in its children. The rhyme originated about a hundred years ago in England, when children used to spend much of their time watching ladybirds run about on the hop vines, searching for food. The children thought that the beetles lived there and so, when the farmers burned the hop vines, as they did every year, the children believed that the young ladybirds and their homes were being destroyed.

The Honeybee

Nearly everyone, from the ancient Egyptians to present-day engineers, has been impressed by the activities of the honeybee. The organization of the hive and the terrific energy of the bees themselves have been a source of wonder and amazement to man for hundreds of years.

The dark interior of a beehive is the centre of many different activities. Although one hive may contain as many as 50,000 inhabitants, there is no confusion. Each bee performs tasks that are necessary for the survival of the whole colony. Most of the honeybees in a hive are worker bees. As their name suggests, these bees gather the nectar and pollen, make the wax honeycombs and care for the young bees. Although the worker bees are constantly busy at these many tasks, they alone could not keep the colony going for very long because they cannot lay eggs that will hatch into workers. In every productive hive there is one bee called the queen. She does nothing but lay eggs.

The queen lays more than 3,000 eggs per day—unfertilized eggs for males (drones) and fertilized for females (workers and future queens). Her welfare is the constant care of the workers, and she is fed a 'royal jelly'. Honey is stored in special cells for the support of the colony throughout the winter, when the drones or male bees are driven out of the hive to die.

For many years men have provided artificial homes for honeybees and in return have taken honey and beeswax. Beeswax is used in many articles, from gramophone records to candles. The sticky golden liquid known as honey was probably the first sugar used by man. When you buy a pound of pure honey, it is hard to realize all the effort that goes into its production, but if you watch one of the worker bees for several hours, you might discover some of the facts about honey-making.

When one of the worker bees leaves the hive to search for the nectar from which honey is made, it will probably cover several miles before it returns. Upon finding a flower from which nectar can be obtained, the worker hovers for a second and then alights, and moves across the petal of the flower until it finds the source of the sweet nectar. Using its tongue, which acts as a sucking tube, the bee draws the nectar into its honey-bag or crop. When it has exhausted the nectar supply of one flower, it flies on to another until its crop is full.

On the flight back to the hive, many different substances in the bee's body are already at work, changing the nectar into honey.

Upon its return to the hive, the worker bee is met by several young workers, and the nectar, which now resembles very watery honey, is transferred to them. These bees then seem to mix the honey by forcing it in and out of their bodies several times. After this, the honey is ready to be stored in a wax cell and left until the excess water has evaporated. When the honey is thick and golden, the bees place a cap of wax over the cell, sealing it until the honey is to be used for food during the winter.

Why do bees buzz, and why do they sting?

The bee's buzz is made by the movement of its wings. The wings vibrate very rapidly, as they move to and fro, and these vibrations set up waves in the air that carry the sound to our ears.

A bee stings to protect itself or a hive from danger. It is the worker bee which has this duty of protecting the community. The stinger, a long, hollow tube with a barb at the tip, grows out from the rear of the insect's body. When the bee needs to protect itself, a drop of poison is forced down the tube, the barb is driven into the enemy and the poison is discharged.

A bee can sting only once, as a general rule, for when it tries to withdraw its stinger, the barb usually breaks off. Sometimes the stinger is so roughly torn from the bee's body that it dies. But the queen bee's stinger does not have a barb, and she can use it again and again to sting rival queens. The drone has no stinger. There are several sting-less bees, but some have a sharp bite.

Miniature Insects

I nsects are among the smallest animals we notice around us. Yet the small body of an insect contains a brain, heart, muscles and other organs that function like those in the complicated body of an animal with a bony skeleton. Each kind of insect is equipped for living in a specific type of environment, and yet all this special equipment is packed in such a small body that we must use a microscope to examine the structure of most insects. It is not that insects cannot be bigger—the stick insect, found in India and other tropical countries, can be as much as a foot long, and millions of years ago there were dragonflies with bodies two feet long. The wonder is that there can be complex creatures so very small, yet perfect in every detail.

There are even pygmy species in insect families too. Grasshoppers are generally quite big insects, just as man is one of the larger kinds of mammal. And, just as the pygmies are a group much smaller than the human average, so pygmy locusts are very small members of the grasshopper family—only half-an-inch long.

A half-inch is about medium size for an insect. Most of the thousands of species that have been discovered so far are less than a half-inch long, and many are so tiny that they look like bits of moving dust to the human eye. Most flies, for instance, are rather small insects, and the tiny biting gnat is about as small as anyone can imagine. Its fiery bite is certainly out of all proportion to its size, which is no larger than a pencil dot.

What is probably the smallest insect in the world is a European wasp, only one-tenth as big as a gnat. This is so very small that even the sharpest human eyes need the aid of a microscope to see it. However, living unnoticed all around us are many of its important cousins which, though twice as big, can barely be seen. These are named the egg-parasites.

Naturally, all members of this family of wasps have to be extremely small, since they lay their eggs in the eggs of other insects—in this way, they make sure of a food supply for their young, and also prove themselves good friends of the farmers.

This minute species is valuable to us because it so often selects the eggs of butterflies and moths whose caterpillars destroy our farm crops. The wasp larvae are parasites, hatching and growing inside the moth egg at the expense of the caterpillar, which dies before it can hatch and start damaging plants. In seven weeks, three female wasps of one species can have about 300,000 descendants, and so, uncountable thousands may be living on a single farm.

Since there are egg-parasite wasps in all parts of the world where crops of grain, cotton and fruit grow, we are very fortunate to have them on our side in our struggle for more food.

Some Insect Giants

While insects do not compete in size with the higher animals, there are many species—giants of their class—which grow to impressive proportions. The largest insects that ever lived were the huge ancestors of our dragonflies, which in prehistoric times darted over the streams and pools of primeval forests. The impression of their wings and bodies preserved in the limestone rocks of the Carboniferous period have provided us with a record of their appearance. The largest of these insects measured two feet across its expanded wings. Our present-day dragonflies have a wing expanse of about six inches. They are small compared to their ancestors, and are harmless, except to the insects they prey on.

Of all the curious and weirdly constructed creatures which are to be found in the world perhaps the strangest are the Phasmids, commonly known as stick and leaf insects. Their variety of form can hardly be surpassed. Some are like walking blades of grass, their bodies and limbs reduced to mere lines. Others are heavier in build, and imitate withered twigs. Others again have their bodies flattened out in the form of a leaf and impressed with veins and a midrib. So complete is the resemblance to a leaf that it is impossible to recognize the creatures except when they move.

The largest of the stick insects in India is a giant, measuring eighteen inches in length from its head to the top of its abdomen. Its body looks and is coloured like a withered twig, while its sprawling ungainly legs help to heighten the resemblance. It is found in Assam and in the rainswept forests of southern India.

Quite as remarkable as the stick insects are the mantis or praying insects. They are often uninvited guests at the dining table. The most familiar and perhaps the largest of the tribe is a robust green fellow about six inches long. His soft leaf-shaped abdomen is concealed under overlapping gauzy wings. His strong spiny forelegs, held over his head like two arms outstretched in prayer, are his most striking features. Hence the name praying mantis.

A mantis will rest motionless on its perch for several hours, waiting for some small insect to come its way. Squatting on two pairs of legs, its foreparts held erect, the mantis watches and waits. It turns its head a little from side to side, attentively. An insect settles nearby. The mantis stiffens its body. Its head is held rigid, while its arms gradually reach out. Slowly and deliberately it advances within striking distance, and strikes quickly and vigorously. The victim is seized and held by the spiny arms, carried to the mouth and eaten.

There are several giant grasshoppers, among them the 'Bherwa', common in Bihar, a bulky, wingless and rather unpleasant-looking creature, with an alarming mouth, long waving horns and sturdy legs. It lives in loose sandy soil, generally in the banks of rivers where it digs itself into a deep burrow.

The beetle tribe has produced a few monsters, including the elephant beetle, the rhinoceros beetle, the stag beetle and the bamboo beetle. Other giants are the 'Goliath' from West Africa, and the West Indian 'Hercules'. The largest butterflies are the swallowtails. The largest moth in India is the atlas moth, which has a wing expanse of ten–twelve inches. It lives in our hill forests and is a most beautiful and vividly coloured insect.

In spite of their limitations in size, insects are dominant creatures which have increased and multiplied and almost possessed the earth. Their smallness in relation to other animals has been a distinct advantage to them.

They are fast to develop, and faster to reproduce. The descendants of a single pair of flies produced within the space of a year runs into many thousands. Then again, thousands of insects can concentrate upon one point where food is aplenty, and in times of stress can scatter over wide areas, while large animals like sheep and cows, when faced with scarcity, die of starvation.

This is why insects are able to make such a success of the business of living. Mere bulk does not protect a species: rapid increase will. Thousands may perish in adversity, but some will survive to carry on the race.

Music in the Trees

I n India, the monsoon is the season when our insect orchestra is at its best. It is true that the shrill music of the cicada is heard throughout the hot weather; but theirs is a prelude to the great concert that comes into full play once the rainy season begins. When the monsoon with its magic touch brings life and greenness to rock and earth and tree, the whole air seems to come alive with the music of insects. Grasshoppers shrill in the bushes, crickets chirp from under stones, and in the water-laden fields there are hundreds of minor artists providing a medley of sounds.

Amongst our more vocal and better-known insect musicians are those that dwell in trees, the cicadas and the crickets. As musicians, the cicadas are in a class by themselves. Most of the species in India are forest dwellers, but there are some who inhabit the open country in the plains. All through the hot weather their chorus rings through the jungle, while a shower of rain, far from damping their spirits, only rouses them to a deafening, combined effort. The ancient Greeks knew the cicada well. They appreciated his music so much that they kept him captive in a cage to sing. Only the males were chosen, for the females, like most insect musicians, were completely dumb. This moved one of the Greek poets to exclaim, 'Happy are the cicadas, for they have voiceless wives.'

The cicada's sound-producing organs are amongst the most remarkable in the animal kingdom. The underside of his body carries a pair of flaps, each of which covers an oval membrane, which looks like the head of a drum. These are set into motion by a great pair of muscles attached to them from within the body, and the sound is produced by their vibration. The whole abdomen, which is practically hollow, helps to increase or diminish the sound.

Simple, isn't it? To be truthful, I find it extremely complicated, and am able to describe the process only by consulting the notes of S.H. Prater, one-time curator of the Bombay Natural History Society.

Let it be added that the female carries these structures in a modified form, but as she has no muscles to bring them into play, she is unable to use them. This is why she must remain silent while her spouse shrieks away. I would change the line from that Greek poet (Xenarchos, I think) and say instead: 'Pity the female cicadas, for they have singing husbands!'

The object of the cicadas' mirthful music is a mystery. It may attract the opposite sex, or it may be just a diversion of the male. Or perhaps he sings because he is happy.

The tree crickets are a band of willing artists who commence their performance as soon as it is dusk. Their sounds are familiar, but the crickets are seldom seen. If one of them enters the house and treats us to a solo, the sound is so surprisingly loud that we can hardly believe it is being produced by so small a creature.

The common Indian tree cricket is a delicate pale-green little creature with hazy, transparent green wings. In full song he holds his wings outspread over his back. They vibrate so rapidly that they are but a blurred outline. A tap on the bush or leaf on which he sits will put an immediate stop to his performance. His music ceases, and he lowers his wings and folds them flat on his back. The grasshopper makes his music by rubbing his legs against his forewing.

I won't go into detail over how the cricket produces its music, except to say that its louder notes are produced by a rapid vibration of the wings, the right wing usually working over the left, the edge of one acting on the file of the other to produce a shrill, long-sustained note.

One of the best-known crickets is a large black fellow who lives underground and rarely comes out by day, except when the rains flood him out of his burrow. But when night falls, he sits on his doorstep and pours out his soul in a strident song. This cricket's name is as impressive as his sound—*Brachytrypes portentosus.*

The mole cricket is a genius by itself. Mole crickets are tillers of the soil. They use their powerful forelimbs for shovelling up the earth and their hard heads for butting into it. Notwithstanding its earthy occupations, the mole cricket is sometimes moved to creating music. But as he repeats his note, a solemn deep-toned chirp, about a hundred times a minute, the performance can be monotonous.

In India, the cone-headed katydids are probably the most notable performers. Katydids are trim, slender grasshopper-like insects, much in evidence in the fresh green grass of the monsoon. In the fields the loud, shrill notes of the males may be heard both by day and by night. Sometimes one of them comes into a house and treats its occupants to a sudden outburst of high-pitched fiddling. His song rises in pitch as the performer warms to his work. In a room it can be quite deafening, and the sound is always difficult to locate—it seems to come from everywhere.

Finally we come to the tree crickets, a band of willing artistes who commence their performance at dusk. Their sounds are familiar, but it is difficult to see the musicians. Presumably the males sing in order to attract their more silent females. The music advertises the presence of the male, just as in other creatures it is the colour or smell that does the job. And if music be the food of love, play on, cicada!

Why are grasshoppers and crickets such persistent little singers? Do they really sing to charm and attract the females, or is their song the voice of mirth? A curious habit has been noticed among certain tree crickets, which may offer a clue to the mystery. Sometimes, as a male sings, a female steals up to him from behind. The male ceases his music. He sits quite still with his wings uplifted. The female noses about his back and soon discovers the object of her search—a deep cavity situated just behind the base of his wings. This cavity contains a clear liquid which she eagerly laps up. Well, even the human male seeks to please his sweetheart with the offer of chocolates.

It is supposed that in this instance the lady is attracted rather by the sweets the male has to offer than by his music. But the music advertises his whereabouts. She hears his sound and knows that he has a sweet nectar to offer her and comes after it. If the artful luring of the male sometimes results in mating, we see the real reason for the male possessing his musical instruments, and understand his urge to play them so continuously. After all, the luring of the female with music and sweets is even practised by human beings. It may not always succeed in its purpose. Sometimes, as with the crickets, the female accepts the gifts so generously offered—and then takes her leave!

Ants and Ant Lions

Red ants may be small, but it is not difficult to find them because they will soon let you know of their presence by their fiery bite.

This notorious (but quite useful) ant lives in trees and makes a nest of leaves, which it fastens together in a very clever manner. The adult ant possesses no material with which to fix up the leaves, but the immature ant-grub or 'larva' has glands that give out a sticky substance, and adult ants make use of this much as we use a gum-bottle. Several ants hold the leaves together whilst others, each seizing a grub and holding it between their forelegs, use it as a living gum-bottle to wet the edges of the leaves, which are then pressed together by the ants holding them.

If you examine such a nest closely (not too closely!) you will find that it is humming with red-ant life. This little ant is a terrific feeder, and will carry away almost any scrap of refuse that he finds. He guards his nest very carefully, and any intruder is attacked by a number of worker-ants, each inflicting a very painful sting. The red ant is useful to man because it lives on insect parasites in fields as well as in godowns. It collects and destroys termites (or 'white ants,' which eat through everything from oak cupboards to Persian carpets) and bedbugs. Some people, of course, might prefer having bugs rather than red ants in their beds!

Incidentally, in Kanara and some other parts of South India, and throughout Burma and Thailand, a paste is made of the red ant, which is eaten as a condiment with curry.

Some of you may have noticed lines of black ants walking up the stem of a tree or plant whilst others are descending—all of them equally in a great hurry. They are after the tiny green, black or brown insects, the blights or aphis, which feed on the sweet sugary sap of the plant, drawing it in through the mouth and passing it out at the other end of the body. They spend their lives doing this.

Ants are very fond of sugar (you must have found them in your sugar bowl often enough), and an ant will make use of a blight in much the same way that a small boy will make use of a stick of sugarcane. The blight has two little tubes passing through the body, and if the insect is pressed from outside a little sugary liquid exudes from the tubes. The clever ant knows this, and with his feelers he drums on the back of the insect, causing the sugary liquid to rise and overflow from the tubes. This is sucked up by the ant until the blight or aphis runs temporarily dry.

The process is similar to our own method of milking a cow. Some communities of ants keep certain kinds of blights in their nests, using them in the same way that we use cows and goats.

Ants are hard-working, serious-minded little fellows, and you will never find them wasting their time. They will store up grain against hard times in the winter, taking it into their nests or heaping it into piles outside the entrance.

The ant has a deadly enemy in the ant lion, a small insect with a very strong pair of jaws. Many small insects have met their death by falling into the cleverly built traps made by ant lions.

The ant lion is only half-an-inch long. Its short, squat body is a dirty grey colour that makes it almost invisible in the sand where it lives. As soon as it hatches from the egg, it starts looking for a place to build its trap.

A sheltered spot is ideal, so that the sand will not be dampened by rain or blown away by the wind. When the ant lion has selected a site, it begins to scoop out a small circular pit in the sand. It uses the end of its body like a small plough, and tosses the sand outside with a jerk of its flat head. When it has finished digging its funnel-shaped pit, it buries itself in the sand at the bottom and lies in wait for some unwary insect. It will wait quietly for hours or even days, its two hollow, curved jaws the only things sticking up out of the sand.

Once a small insect is caught by these powerful jaws, there is little hope of escape, for the ant lion quickly drains away the fluids from the insect and throws the empty skeleton out of the pit. Then it retreats into the sand to wait for its next victim.

Eventually, the ant lion weaves a small ball of silk about itself and changes into a graceful winged adult that looks something like a small dragonfly.

Walk Tall

You stride through the long grass
Pressing on over fallen pine needles,
Up the winding road to the mountain pass:
Small red ant, now crossing a sea
Of raindrops; your destiny
To carry home that single, slender
Cosmos seed,
Waving it like a banner in the sun.

Scorpions

Scorpions are creatures with an evil reputation, and deaths from scorpion stings do sometimes occur in India; but in most cases the victims have been either children or women in weak health condition. Scorpions may live under stones or fallen tree trunks, in deep burrows dug in the soil or in shallow holes in sand, and sometimes in shoes or slippers. There are over 350 different species of scorpions in the world, and India provides a home for at least eighty of them.

One of our best-known species is the common red scorpion, found in the dry regions of Punjab and throughout northern, central and southern India, except in the extreme south. It has a reddish-brown body, yellowish legs and a robust yellow tail with sting attached.

Another common species is the rock scorpion, one of the largest in the world, a black and hairy beast which grows to a length of about eight inches. It walks with its belly touching the ground, and usually drags its great tail behind it. The red scorpion, on the other hand, raises its body high on its legs and curls its tail over its back. In its swifter movements the tail is trailed behind.

Scorpions feed mainly on insects. How such an agile, wary creature as the cockroach allows itself to be caught by the slow-moving, short-sighted scorpion is a marvel. But the life of a cockroach, when it encounters a scorpion, is brief. It either panics and stumbles over the crouching scorpion, or starts inspecting it with its long feelers. The scorpion's pincered arms reach out, and the cockroach is firmly in their grip. Over comes the deadly tail, and the victim is stabbed to death.

A large insect, like a cockroach, is not killed immediately; but the venom paralyses its muscles and leaves it helpless. A reckless stab against the horny covering of an insect like the beetle might easily break the point of the scorpion's sting. That is why the tail is usually carried up or raised from the ground, to keep the sting from being damaged.

Not much is known about the private habits of scorpions, but the great French naturalist, Jean Henri Fabre, established a colony of scorpions in his garden, observed them closely and gave a fascinating account of their courtship and mating habits.

After circling round each other, the male and female stood face-to-face with raised tails. These they intertwined in a friendly embrace. This was followed by a solemn dance. The couple held hands: the male seized the pincers of the female in his own, walking backwards, while she followed him modestly. Backwards and forwards they continued for about an hour, until at length the male began to dig a hole, but without leaving his hold of the female. A home prepared, he dragged her 'over the threshold'.

His mastery over his spouse is only limited to the period of courtship. The male scorpion is often seized and eaten by the female soon after mating: a custom that is also popular with spiders, but not, as yet, amongst humans.

The Spider in Her Parlour

Where do the flies go in the cold weather? There are various opinions. Some entomologists think that they hibernate in warm corners, others hold that the adult flies all die and only the larvae survive into the following spring. Whatever the truth may be, it is known that just one pair of houseflies could, in a single summer, become the ancestors of the staggering total of 191 million million million more of their objectionable kind! Fortunately, only a small proportion of their descendants survive, the rest surrendering to famine, disease and their natural enemies— our friends—the spiders.

A spider's web can be relied upon to catch flies as efficiently as the best flypaper. But ants, bees and wasps, who have a memory and use it, are not usually trapped. Flies belong to a lower order and have no memory and the fact that a fly has struggled free, escaping very narrowly with its life, will not prevent that same fly from getting caught again soon after. Ants, on the other hand, will go to great trouble to rescue a nest-companion, and have even been known to bring fine sand and scatter it across flypaper to make a path to their companion in distress.

Any insect caught in a spider's web stands very little chance of escape, because the sticky web holds it captive until the owner returns. Then she (we will assume it is a female spider since the males though quite plentiful, are small, weak by comparison and less likely to be seen) spins more and more silk over her victim until it cannot even move, when she stings the helpless creature to death with her fangs.

All spiders have fangs; they are therefore held in great respect by most members of the insect world (to which they do not belong, having eight legs) since their bite to them is deadly. Towards humans, of course, the spider has no harmful intent, and there are only a few rare kinds which are poisonous.

One of the most dangerous is the bird-eating spider, found in the West Indies and tropical South America. Being arboreal, it is often found in a banana tree, where it constructs a thick untidy web. Its normal prey consists of large insects, although it welcomes small mammals and birds if they become entangled. As large as a saucer when full-grown, the bird-eating spider moves quickly and inflicts a vicious and poisonous bite, which is sometimes fatal to humans.

However, to return to our more common and harmless

house spiders, they are shy creatures and come out mainly at night—which is why we see so few of them, though their numbers are vast. They are carnivorous or meat-eating animals and will tackle almost anything, provided it is alive—even each other. Indeed, the courtship of his mate is a very risky thing to the male spider who, if he escapes intact, is lucky. Baby spiders can be seen scurrying away from their mother as fast as their legs will take them, and those which hatch after they are born soon learn to keep their distance from each other. For this reason, attempts to produce spider-silk commercially have failed. Unlike the familiar silkworm, they simply cannot be persuaded to live sufficiently close together.

As I have said, spiders are not insects: they have two legs too many, their head and thorax is complete in one (no join at the neck) and they never have wings. Even so, some spiders can fly. They climb to the top of a high post and send out long lines of silk which, when caught by the wind, act as kites. The little creatures cast themselves off when the tug is just right and can fly in this way for many miles and at great heights. They have been found by research aeroplanes at altitudes of 5,000 feet—nearly a mile in the air!

Nor are these the only purposes to which the spider puts her silk. One American spider chooses a good position, such as the end of a branch, and spins out a long line, which she weights with a ball of the same stuff. She then flings this at any tiny insect flying her way and hauls in her catch. She never sticks to it herself, because of a special oil her body makes to protect her.

Insects in Disguise

Curious as the mantis or praying insects are, their present appearance has probably come about through a continuous series of minute changes that enable them to obtain their prey (which consists chiefly of other insects) with greater ease. They are heavy and clumsy on the wing, and sometimes they are wingless. These insects have discovered that by imitating the colour and characteristics of their surroundings, they have a better chance of capturing their prey.

The foliage-dwelling mantises have acquired a vivid tint of green, with perhaps yellowish and brownish markings, which enable them to lie unnoticed on a leaf or green twig till some unwary insect comes their way; and there are other, banded or spotted species, which are usually found amongst flowers.

Have you ever watched a mantis hunting? Only the two hind pairs of legs are used for walking. On them he heaves over very slowly so that the movement is scarcely noticeable; and then, just as his centre of gravity is almost lost, out shoots a leg with amazing swiftness. Another gradual heaving over of the body, and another lightning movement of the leg. And so he advances step by step until the prey is within reaching distance of the mantis's terrible forelegs. There is no escape from those forelegs once they close round a lesser insect.

Each of the forelegs is equipped with sharp spiky teeth or spines, set backwards like a saw. The position in which these legs are held is one of prayer (hence its name), but peaceful prayer is the last thing the mantis has in mind. He tears his victims to pieces, and feeds upon them while they are still struggling.

The mantis uses his camouflage to deceive his prey, and also to protect himself from dangerous enemies. There is also a type of camouflage known as warning colouration. The banded krait affords a good example of this type of colouration. It is a fairly large snake, sometimes reaching a length of six feet, and marked all along the length of its body with alternate rings of black and pale yellow. Another species, the red-headed krait, has a black body and bright scarlet head and tail. Both snakes are dangerously poisonous, but the primary purpose of their venom is to paralyse their prey. It is of little use as a weapon of defence, because its action is slow. A man bitten by a krait may die some hours afterwards, but at the time he is bitten he has plenty of time in which to kill the snake before the venom starts having an effect on him. The same is true of any fairly large animal that attacks a krait. It is therefore to the snake's advantage to proclaim its dangerous nature and so discourage larger animals from attacking.

Many kinds of wasps are striped with yellow and black, a pattern that advertises their ability to sting. And there are striking examples of warning colouration among certain tropical frogs, which have glands secreting a poison likely to cause the death of any animal that tries to eat them. Some of these frogs are brightly patterned with black and red, or black and yellow. One of them, a South American variety, is in fact used by the aborigines to make poison.

Section 2

Birdsong in the Mountains

At the Bird Bath

A whistling thrush comes to bathe in the rainwater puddle beneath the window. He loves this spot. So now, when there is no rain, I fill the puddle with water, so that my favourite bird keeps coming.

His bath finished, he perches on a branch of the walnut tree. His glossy blue-back wings glitter in the sunshine. At any moment he will start singing.

Here he goes! He tries out the tune, whistling to himself, and then, confident of the notes, sends his trilling, full-throated voice far over the forest. The song dies down, trembling, lingering in the air; starts again, joyfully, and then suddenly stops, as though the singer had forgotten the words or the tune.

A little distance from my home, a number of small birds bathe and drink in the little pool beneath the cherry tree: hunting parties of tits—grey tits, red-headed tits and green-backed tits, and two delicate little willow-warblers. They take turns in the pool. While the green-backs are taking a plunge, the red-heads wait patiently on the moss-covered rocks, coming down later to sip daintily at the edge of the pool; they don't like getting their feet wet! Finally, when they have all gone away, the whistling thrush arrives and indulges in an orgy of bathing, as he now has the entire pool to himself.

The babblers are adept at snapping up the little garden skinks that scuttle about in the leaves and the grass. The skinks are quite brittle and are easily broken to pieces with a few hard raps of the beak. Then down they go! Babblers are also good at sifting through dead leaves and seizing upon various insects.

A Wilderness
in New Delhi

If you are determined, you can find a wilderness close to you, no matter where you live. In 1959, I was living on the outskirts of a greater, further New Delhi. The influx of refugees from the Punjab after Partition had led to many new colonies springing up on the outskirts of the capital, and at the time, the furthest of these was Rajouri Garden. Needless to say, there were no gardens. The treeless colony was buffeted by hot, dusty winds from Haryana and Rajasthan. The houses were built on one side of Najafgarh Road. On the other side, as yet uncolonized, were extensive fields of wheat and other crops still belonging to the original inhabitants. In an attempt to escape the city life that constantly oppressed me, I would walk across the main road and into the fields, finding old wells, irrigation channels, camels and buffaloes, and sighting birds and small creatures that no longer dwelt in the city life, which led to my taking a greater interest in the natural world. Up to that time, I had taken it all for granted. The notebook I kept at the time lies before me now, and my first entry describes the blue jays or rollers that were much a feature of those remaining open spaces. At rest, the bird is fairly nondescript, but when it takes flight it reveals the glorious bright blue wings and the tail, banded with a lighter blue. It sits motionless, but the large dark eyes are constantly watching the ground in every direction. A grasshopper or cricket has only to make a brief appearance, and the blue jay will launch itself straight at its prey. In spring and early summer the 'roller' lives up to its other name. It indulges in love flights, in which it rises and falls in the air with harsh grating screams—a real rock 'n' roller!

Some way down the Najafgarh Road was a large village pond and beside it a magnificent banyan tree. We have no place for banyan trees today, they need so much space in which to spread their limbs and live comfortably. Cut away its aerial roots and the great tree topples over—usually to make way for a spacious apartment building. That was the first banyan tree I got to know well. It had about a hundred pillars supporting the boughs, and above them there was a great leafy crown like a pillared hall. It has been said that whole armies could shelter in the shade of an old banyan. And probably at one time they did. I saw another sort of army visit the banyan by the village pond when it was in fruit. Parakeets, mynas, rosy pastors, crested bulbuls without crests, barbets and many other birds crowded the tree in order to feast noisily on big scarlet figs. Even further down the Najafgarh Road was a large jheel, famous for its fishing. I wonder if any part of the jheel still exists, or if it got filled in and became a part of greater Delhi. One could rest in the shade of a small babul or keekar tree and watch the kingfisher skim over the water, making just a slight splash as it dived and came up with small glistening fish. Our common Indian kingfisher is a beautiful little bird with a brilliant blue back, a white throat and orange underparts. I would spot one perched on an overhanging bush or rock, and wait to see it plunge like an arrow into the water and return to its perch to devour the catch. It came over the water in a flash of gleaming blue, shrilling its loud 'tit-tit-tit'. The kingfisher is the subject of a number of legends, and the one I remember best, recounted by Romain Rolland, tells us that it was originally a plain grey bird that acquired its resplendent colours by flying straight towards the sun when Noah let it out of the ark. Its upper plumage took the colour of the sky above, while the lower was scorched a deep russet by the rays of the setting sun. Summer and winter, I scorned the dust and the traffic, and walked all over Delhi, in search of quiet spots with some shade, a few birds, flower and fruit. I spent many afternoons lying on the grass near India Gate and eating jamuns. I liked the sour tang of the jamun fruit, which was best eaten with a little salt. And I liked the deep purple colour of the fruit. Jamuns were one of the nicer things about Delhi.

A Bush at Hand Is Good for Many a Bird

The thing I like most about shrubs and small bushes is that they are about my size or thereabouts. I can meet them on equal terms. Most trees grow tall, they overtake us after a few years, and we find ourselves looking up to them with a certain amount of awe and deference. And so we should.

A bush, on the other hand, may have been in the ground a long time—thirty or forty years or more—while continuing to remain a bush, man-sized and approachable. A bush may spread sideways or gain in substance, but it seldom towers over you. This means that I can be on intimate terms with it, know its qualities—of leaf, bud, flower, birds, small mammals or reptiles. Of course, we know that bushes are ideal for binding the earth together and preventing erosion. In this respect they are just as important as trees. Every monsoon I witness landslides all about me, but I know the hillside just above my cottage is well-knit, knotted and netted, by the bilberry and raspberry, wild jasmine, dog rose and bramble, and other shrubs, vines and creepers.

I have made a small bench in the middle of this civilized wilderness. And sitting here, I can look down on my own roof, as well as sideways and upwards, into a number of bushes, teeming with life throughout the year. This is my favourite place. No one can find me here, unless I call out and make my presence known. The buntings and sparrows, 'grown accustomed to my face' and welcoming the grain I scatter for them, flit about near my feet. One of them, bolder than the rest, alights on my shoes and proceeds to polish his beak on the leather. The sparrows are here all year round. So are the whistling thrushes, who live in the shadows between house and hill, sheltered by a waterwood bush, so cared because it likes cool, damp places.

Summer brings the fruit-eating birds, for now that the berries are ripe, a pair of green pigeons, rare in these parts, scramble over the branches of a hawthorn bush, delicately picking off the fruit. The raspberry bush is raided by bands of finches and greedy yellow-bottomed bulbuls. A flock of bright green parrots comes swooping down on a medlar tree, but they do not stay for long. Taking flight at my approach, they wheel above, green and gold in the sunlight, and make for the plum trees further down the road. The kingora, a native Himalyan shrub similar to the bilberry, attracts small boys as well as birds. On their way to and from school, the boys scramble up the hillside and help themselves to the small sweet-and-sour berries. Then, lips stained purple, they go their merry way. The birds return.

Roosting in the Semul

The semul is as remarkable for the colour and profusion of its flowers as for the large number of birds that visit it when it is in flower. Some birds come for nectar that is found in the big, red flowers; some come in search of the thousands of drowned insects that lie at the bottom of the flower cups; some come because the soft wood of the tree can easily be hollowed out for a nesting site. Whatever the reason, from morning till night the tree is full of visitors.

Among those who visit the semul are a large number of crows, who come to have a few sips of the nectar before setting out on the day's mischief. There are mynas of various kinds, squabbling for the best seats. Barbets and bulbuls, king crows and koels, all join in the feasting. In addition to the birds, palm squirrels dart about from place to place, tossing their fluffy tails from side to side, and chattering noisily as they jostle each other on the branches. And all the time flowers are being constantly broken off, falling to the ground with soft thuds.

The rosy pastors or rose-coloured starlings are probably the most noticeable visitors to the semul tree. They come in flocks, not singly; their colour vies with that of the flowers; they make such a racket that one thinks that a terrible riot is going on. But the pastors are not fighting, they are simply enjoying themselves.

Another inhabitant of the semul tree is the big Indian bee. This bee lives in huge nests, or combs, which are usually attached to the branches of the semul tree. The straight horizontal branches of the semul are just right for supporting the huge combs, which can be as much as five feet in width. The residents of the comb are of three kinds—the males or drones who do no work, the females who lay the eggs, and the workers who build the giant combs. These are permanent colonies, filled with honey or wax or pollen.

The sting of the big bee is painful and poisonous, especially in hot weather; but jungle tribes, such as the Kols and the Santals, have developed immunity to the poison. They don't mind being stung. But strangers to the forests have been badly stung, and it is wise not to disturb these bees, for they will attack both man and beast with great ferocity.

There is the story of two shikaris who were resting between beats one hot May morning in a central Indian jungle. Overhead spread the crown of a tall semul tree with a dozen great combs of the big bee hanging from the branches. One of the shikaris unwisely lit a pipe. Up went the pipe smoke, and down came the bees! They were soon buzzing around the two shikaris, who beat an undignified retreat, running for over a mile across open country until they reached the safety of a river. They were so badly stung that they had to remain in the river for hours, up to their chins in water.

Birdlife in the City

Having divided the last ten years of my life between Delhi and Mussoorie, I have come to the heretical conclusion that there is more birdlife in the cities than in the hills and forests around our hill stations.

For birds to survive, they must learn to live with, and off, humans; and those birds, like crows, sparrows and mynas, who do this to perfection, continue to thrive as our cities grow; whereas the purely wild birds, those who depend upon the forests for life, are rapidly disappearing, simply because the forests are disappearing.

Recently, I saw more birds in one week in a New Delhi colony than I had seen during a month in the hills. Here, one must be patient and alert if one is to spot just a few of the birds so beautifully described in Salim Ali's *Indian Hill Birds*. The babblers and thrushes are still around, but the flycatchers and warblers are seldom seen or heard.

But in Delhi, if you have just a bit of garden and perhaps a guava tree, you will be visited by innumerable bulbuls, tailorbirds, mynas, hoopoes, parrots and tree pies. Or, if you own an old house, you will have to share it with pigeons and sparrows, perhaps swallows and swifts. And if you have neither garden nor rooftop, you will be visited by the crows.

Where man goes, the crow follows. He has learnt to perfection the art of living off humans. He will, I am sure, be the first bird on the moon, scavenging among the paper bags and cartons left behind by untidy astronauts.

Crows favour the densest areas of human population, and there must be at least one for every human. Many crows seem to have been humans in their previous lives: they possess all the cunning and sense of self-preservation of man. At the same time, there are many humans who have obviously been crows; we haven't lost their thieving instincts.

Watch a crow sidling along the garden wall with a shabby genteel air, cocking a speculative eye at the kitchen door and any attendant humans. He reminds one of a newspaper reporter hovering in the background until his chance comes—and then pouncing! I have even known a crow to make off with an off from the breakfast table. No other bird, except perhaps the sparrow, has been so successful in exploiting human beings.

The myna, although he too is quite at home in the city, is more of a gentleman. He prefers fruit on the tree to scraps from the kitchen, and visits the garden as much out of a sense of sociability as in expectation of hand-outs. He is quite handsome, too, with his bright orange bill and the mask around his eyes. He is equally at home on a railway platform as on the ear of a grazing buffalo, and being omnivorous, has no trouble in coexisting with man.

The sparrow, on the other hand, is not a gentleman. Uninvited, he enters your home, followed by his friends, relatives and political hangers-on, and proceeds to quarrel, make love and leave his droppings on the sofa-cushions, with a complete disregard for the presence of humans. The party will then proceed into the garden and destroy all the flower-buds. No birds have succeeded so well in making fools of humans.

Although the blue jay, or roller, is quite capable of making his living in the forest, he seems to show a preference for the haunts of men, would rather perch on a telegraph wire than in a tree. Probably he finds the wire a better launching-pad for his sudden rocket-flights and aerial acrobatics.

In repose he is rather shabby; but in flight, when his outspread wings reveal his brilliant blues, he takes one's breath away. As his food consists of beetles and other insect pests, he can be considered man's friend and ally.

Parrots make little or no distinction between town and country life. They are the freelancers of the bird world—study, independent and noisy. With flashes of blue and green, they swoop across the road, settle for a while in a mango tree, and then, with shrill delighted cries, move on to some other field or orchard.

They will sample all the fruit they can, without finishing any. They are destructive birds, but because of their bright plumage, graceful flight and charming ways, they are popular favourites and can get away with anything. No one who has enjoyed watching a flock of parrots in swift and carefree flight would want to cage one of these virile birds. Yet so many people do cage them.

After the peacock, perhaps the most popular bird in rural India is the sarus crane—a familiar sight around the jheels and river banks of northern India and Gujarat. The sarus pairs for life and is seldom seen without his mate. When one bird dies, the other often pines away and seemingly dies of grief. It is this near-human quality of devotion that has earned the birds their popularity with the villagers of the plains.

As a result, they are well-protected.

In the long run, it is the 'common man', and not the scientist or conservationist, who can best give protection to the birds and animals living around him. Religious sentiment has helped preserve the peacock and few other birds. It is a pity that so many other equally beautiful birds do not enjoy the same protection.

But the wily crow, the cheeky sparrow and the sensible myna, will always be with us. Quite possibly they will survive the human species.

Owls in the Family

One winter morning, my grandfather and I found a baby spotted owlet by the veranda steps of our home in Dehradun. When Grandfather picked it up the owlet hissed and clacked its bill but then, after a meal of, raw meat and water, settled down under my bed.

Spotted owlets are small birds. A fully grown one is no larger than a thrush and they have none of the sinister appearance of large owls. I had once found a pair of them in our mango tree and by tapping on the tree trunk had persuaded one to show an enquiring face at the entrance to its hole. The owlet is not normally afraid of man, nor is it strictly a night bird. But it prefers to stay at home during the day, as it is sometimes attacked by other birds who consider all owls their enemies.

The little owlet was quite happy under my bed. The following day we found a second baby owlet in almost the same spot on the veranda and only then did we realize that where the rainwater pipe emerged through the roof, there was a rough sort of nest from which the birds had fallen. We took the second young owl to join the first and fed them both.

When I went to bed, they were on the window ledge just inside the mosquito netting and later in the night, their mother found them there. From outside, she crooned and gurgled for a long time and in the morning, I found she had left a mouse with its tail tucked through the netting. Obviously she put no great trust in me as a foster parent.

The young birds thrived and ten days later, Grandfather and I took them into the garden to release them. I had placed one on a branch of the mango tree and was stooping to pick up the other when I received a heavy blow on the head. A second or two later, the mother owl swooped down on Grandfather, but he was quite agile and ducked out of the way.

Quickly, I placed the second owl under the mango tree. Then from a safe distance we watched the mother fly down and lead her offspring into the long grass at the edge of the garden. We thought she would take her family away from our rather strange household, but the next morning I found the two owlets perched on the hatstand in the veranda.

I ran to tell Grandfather and when we came back, we found the mother sitting on the birdbath a few metres away. She was evidently feeling sorry for her behaviour the previous day because she greeted us with a soft 'whoo-whoo'.

'Now there's an unselfish mother for you,' said Grandfather. 'It's obvious she wants us to keep an eye on them. They're probably getting too big for her to manage.'

So the owlets became regular members of our household and were among the few pets that Grandmother took a liking to. She objected to all snakes, most monkeys and some crows—we'd had all these pets from time to time—but she took quite a fancy to the owlets and frequently fed them spaghetti!

They loved to sit and splash in a shallow dish provided by Grandmother. They enjoyed it even more if cold water was poured over them from a jug while they were in the bath. They would get thoroughly wet, jump out and perch on a towel rack, shake themselves and return for a second splash and sometimes a third. During the day they dozed on a hatstand. After dark, they had the freedom of the house and their nightly occupation was catching beetles, the kitchen quarters being a happy hunting ground. With razor-sharp eyes and powerful beaks, they were excellent pest-destroyers.

Looking back on those childhood days, I carry in my mind a picture of Grandmother in her rocking chair with a contented owlet sprawled across her aproned lap. Once, on entering a room while she was taking an afternoon nap, I saw one of the owlets had crawled up her pillow till its head was snuggled under her ear. Both Grandmother and the owlet were snoring.

Birds of the Night

Having for a number of years suffered from rather poor vision, I am not the most eagle-eyed of birdwatchers. But, like many who don't see too well, I have good powers of hearing, awakening in the night at the squeak of a mouse or the fluttering of a moth against the window pane. And when, at times, sleep is elusive, I can lie awake and derive pleasure from the sounds and calls of those birds who live largely by night.

Not that all bird-calls are pleasing to the ear. The hawk-cuckoo semitones until one begins to think that the performer must surely burst. But the brainfever bird never bursts. Its cry is repeated for hours at a stretch.

He is a hot-weather bird who haunts the groves and gardens in almost all parts of the country, his range extending from the Himalayan foothills to Cape Comorin. Only Assam and Punjab appear to be free from the attentions of this cuckoo.

Another cuckoo, the common Indian cuckoo, has quite a pleasant note, which may be rendered by the words 'wherefore, wherefore', with quite a musical cadence. It begins to call about two hours before sunset, and continues through the night until the morning hours. It is usually silent during the middle of the day, when presumably it rests its vocal chords.

There is a third night-loving cuckoo, the koel, who, like the brainfever bird, is not very popular with those who must try to sleep within hearing distance. His 'ku-oo' grows more strident with each successive rise in scale until sleep becomes almost impossible for anyone in the vicinity. Cunningham described it as a 'highly pitched, trisyllabic cry, repeated many times in ascending' as, Douglas Dewar wrote, 'the jaded dweller in the plains, uttering strange oaths, rushes for his gun and seeks out the disturber of his slumber.' But the clamour breaks off abruptly, and the sleeper returns to bed, rejoicing in the thought that the wretched bird has choked itself. And it is just then that the bird begins all over again!

Nightjars are not much to look at, although their large, lustrous eyes gleam uncannily in the light of a lamp. But their sounds are distinctive. The breeding call of the Indian nightjar resembles the sound of a stone skimming over the surface of a frozen pond; it can be heard for a considerable distance. Douglas Dewar described the call of the Indian nightjar memorably as 'the sound made by a stone skimming over ice'. Another species utters a loud grating call which, when close at hand, sounds exactly like a whiplash cutting the air. 'Horsfield's nightjar' makes a noise similar to that made by striking a plank with a hammer.

During the day the bird spends long hours sitting motionless on the ground, where it is practically invisible, only springing into life when an intruder approaches. It is also called the 'goatsucker' because of its huge mouth and the legend spread in many countries that it feeds from the udders of cows and goats. Because of this erroneous belief, it is considered a bird of ill omen. Night-flying insects, such as moths and beetles, are its preferred meals.

We mustn't forget the owls, those most celebrated of night birds, much maligned by poets obsessed with death and cemeteries.

Actually the owls have the pleasantest of calls. The little jungle owlet has a note that is both mellow and musical. Then there is the little scops owl, who speaks only in monosyllables, except for an occasional 'wow'.

Probably the most familiar of Indian owls is the spotted owlet. He is really a noisy bird, who pours forth a volley of chuckles and squeaks and chatters in the early evening and at intervals throughout the night. In the daytime, like other owls, the spotted owlet is silent, and hides away in some dark corner, such as a hole in a tree or a wall, emerging towards sunset to hunt a prey—chiefly insects, but also occasionally mice, shrews and lizards.

Towards sunset, I watch the owlets emerge from their holes one after another. Before coming out, each puts out a queer little round head with staring eyes. After they have emerged they usually sit very quietly for a time, as though only half-awake. Then, all of a sudden, they begin to chuckle, finally breaking out in a torrent of chattering. Having in this way 'psyched' themselves into the right frame of mind, they spread their short, rounded wings and sail off for the night's hunting.

Birdsong in the Mountains

Birdwatching is more difficult in the hills than in the plains. It is hard to spot many birds against the dark trees of the varying shades of the hillside.

There are few birds who remain silent for long, however, and one learns of their presence from their calls or songs. Birdsong is with you wherever you go in the Himalayas, from the foothills to the treeline; and it is often easier to recognize a bird from its voice than from its colourful but brief appearance.

The barbet is one of those birds which are heard more often than they are seen. It has a monotonous far-reaching call, 'pee-oh, pee-oh', which carries for about a mile. Like politicians, these birds love listening to their own voices, and often two or three will answer each other from different trees, each trying to outdo the rest in a shrill shouting match. Some people like the barbet's call and consider it both striking and pleasant. Some just find it striking.

Hodgson's grey-headed flycatcher-warbler is a long name that ornithologists, in their infinite wisdom, have given to a very small bird. This tiny warbler is heard, if not seen, more often than any other bird throughout the western Himalayas. Its voice is heard in every second tree, and yet there are few who can say what it looks like. Its song (if you can call it that), is not very tuneful and puts me in mind of the notice that sometimes appeared in salons out West: 'The audience is requested not to throw things at the pianist. He is doing his best.'

Our little warbler does its best, incessantly emitting four or five unmusical, but nevertheless joyful and penetrating, notes.

Another tiny bird heard more often than it is seen is the green-backed tit, a smart little fellow about the size of a sparrow. It utters a sharp, rather metallic, but not unpleasant call which sounds like 'kiss me, kiss me, kiss me'.

A real songster is the grey-winged ouzel, found here in the Garhwal hills. Throughout the early summer it makes the wooded hillsides ring with a melody that Nelson Eddy would have been proud of. Joining in sometimes with a sweet song of its own, is the green pigeon. As though to mock their arias, the laughing-thrushes, who are exponents of heavy rock, give vent to some weird calls of their own.

When I first came to live in the hills, it was the song of the Himalayan whistling thrush that first caught my attention. I was sitting at my window, gazing out at the new leaves on the walnut tree. All was still; the wind was at peace with itself, the mountains brooded massively under a darkening sky. Then, emerging like a sweet secret from the depths of a deep ravine, came this indescribably beautiful call.

It is a song that never fails to enchant me. The bird starts with a hesitant whistle, as though trying out the tune; then, once confident of the melody, it bursts into full song, a crescendo of sweet notes and variations ringing clearly across the hillside. Suddenly the song breaks off, right in the middle of a cadenza, and I am left wondering what happened to make the bird stop. Nothing really, because the song is taken up again a few moments later.

One day I saw the whistling thrush perched on the broken garden fence. He was a deep, glistening purple, his shoulders flecked with white. He has sturdy black legs and a strong yellow beak; a dapper fellow who would have looked just right in a top hat. As time passed, he 'grew accustomed to my face' and became a regular visitor to the garden. On sultry summer afternoons I would find him flapping about in the water tank. Later, refreshed and sunning himself on the roof, he would treat me to a little concert before flying off to his shady ravine.

It was a boy from the next village who acquainted me with the legend of the whistling thrush. According to the story, the young god Krishna fell asleep near a stream, and while he slept a small boy made off with Krishna's famous flute. Upon waking and finding his flute gone, Krishna was so angry that he changed the culprit into a bird. But having once played the flute, the boy had learnt bits and pieces of the god's enchanting music. And so he continued, in his disrespectful way, to play the music of the gods, only stopping now and then (as the whistling thrush does) when he couldn't remember the tune.

It wasn't long before my whistling thrush was joined by a female. Sometimes they gave solo performances, sometimes they sang duets; and these latter notes, no doubt, were love calls, because it wasn't long before the pair were making forays into the rocky ledges of the ravine, looking for a suitable nesting site.

The birds were liveliest in midsummer; but even in the depths of winter, with snow lying on the ground, they would suddenly start singing, as they flitted from pine to oak to naked chestnut.

The wild cherry tree, which grows just outside my bedroom window, attracts a great many small birds, both when it is in flower and when it is in fruit.

When it is covered with small pink blossoms, the most common visitor is a little yellow-backed sunbird, who emits a squeaky little song as she flits from branch to branch. She extracts the nectar from the blossoms with her long tubular tongue.

Amongst other visitors are the flycatchers, gorgeous birds, especially the paradise flycatcher with its long white tail and ghost-like flight. Basically an insect eater, it likes fruits for dessert, and will visit the tree when the cherries are ripening. While moving along the boughs of the tree, they utter twittering notes, with occasional louder calls, and now and then the male breaks into a sweet little song, thus justifying the name shah bulbul (king of the nightingales), by which he is known in northern India.

Guests Who Fly in from the Forest

When mist fills the Himalayan valleys, and heavy monsoon rain sweeps across the hills, it is natural for wild creatures to seek shelter. Any shelter is welcome in a storm—and sometimes my cottage in the forest is the most convenient refuge.

There is no doubt that I make things easier for all concerned by leaving most of my windows open—I am one of those peculiar people who like to have plenty of fresh air indoors—and if a few birds, beasts and insects come in too, they're welcome, provided they don't make too much of a nuisance of themselves.

I must confess that I did not lose patience with a bamboo beetle who blundered in the other night and fell into the water jug. I rescued him and pushed him out of the window. A few seconds later he came whirring in again, and with unerring accuracy, landed with a plop in the same jug. I fished him out once more and offered him the freedom of the night. But attracted no doubt by the light and warmth of my small sitting room, he came buzzing back, circling the room like a helicopter looking for a good place to land. Quickly I covered the water jug. He landed in a bowl of wild dahlias, and I allowed him to remain there, comfortably curled up in the hollow of a flower.

Sometimes, during the day, a bird visits me—a deep purple whistling thrush, hopping about on long dainty legs, peering to right and left, too nervous to sing. She perches on the windowsill, looking out at the rain. She does not permit any familiarity. But if I sit quietly in my chair, she will sit quietly on her windowsill, glancing quickly at me now and then just to make sure that I'm keeping my distance. When the rain stops, she glides away, and it is only then, confident in her freedom, that she bursts into full-throated song, her broken but haunting melody echoing down the ravine.

A squirrel comes sometimes, when his home in the oak tree gets waterlogged. Apparently he is a bachelor; anyway, he lives alone. He knows me well, this squirrel, and is bold enough to climb on to the dining table looking for tidbits which he always finds, because I leave them there deliberately. Had I met him when he was a youngster, he would have learned to eat from my hand; but I have only been here for a few months. I like it this way. I am not looking for pets: these are simply guests.

Last week, as I was sitting down at my desk to write a

long-deferred article, I was startled to see an emerald-green praying mantis sitting on my writing pad. He peered up at me with his protuberant glass-bead eyes, and I started down at him through my reading glasses. When I gave him a prod, he moved off in a leisurely way. Later I found him examining the binding of Whitman's *Leaves of Grass*; perhaps he had found a succulent bookworm. He disappeared for a couple of days, and then I found him on the dressing table, preening himself before the mirror. Perhaps I am doing him an injustice in assuming that he was preening. Maybe he thought he'd met another mantis and was simply trying to make contact. Anyway, he seemed fascinated by his reflection.

Out in the garden, I spotted another mantis, perched on the jasmine bush. Its arms were raised like a boxer's. Perhaps they're a pair, I thought, and went indoors and fetched my mantis and placed him on the jasmine bush, opposite his fellow insect. He did not like what he saw—no comparison with his own image!—and made off in a huff.

My most interesting visitor comes at night, when the lights are still burning—a tiny bat who prefers to fly in at the door, should it be open, and will use the window only if there's no alternative. His object in entering the house is to snap up the moths that cluster around the lamps.

All the bats I've seen fly fairly high, keeping near the ceiling as far as possible, and only descending to ear level (my ear level) when they must; but this particular bat flies in low, like a dive bomber, and does acrobatics amongst the furniture, zooming in and out of chair legs and under tables. Once, while careening about the room in this fashion, he passed straight between my legs. Has his radar gone wrong, I wondered, or is he just plain crazy?

I went to my shelves of *Natural History* and looked up bats, but could find no explanation for this erratic behaviour.

The Whistling Schoolboy

From the gorge above Gangotri
Down to Kochi by the sea,
The whistling thrush keeps singing
His constant melody.

He was a whistling schoolboy once,
Who heard Lord Krishna's flute,
And tried to play the same sweet tune,
But struck a faulty note.

Said Krishna to the erring youth:
A bird you must become,
And you shall whistle all your days,
Until your song is done.

Section 3

The Loveliness of Ferns

The Coconut Tree

T he beginnings of most cultivated plants are a mystery, and few have received as much attention from scientists and botanists as the familiar coconut palm. Though it cannot be proved that the coconut first originated in India, there is no doubt that this tree has been with us since earliest times. Mention is made of it in several of the Puranas, which are the oldest books after the Vedas. There is also mention of it in the Ramayana and the Mahabharata as well as in ancient Tamil literature. In some Hindu ceremonies, worship is offered to Varuna, the god presiding over the water and the oceans. This god is represented by a pot of water with a coconut placed at the mouth. The offering of an unbroken coconut to the sea probably comes from the idea that the coconut came from the seas. And there is a Ceylonese legend that says that it was brought to India from Nagaloka, a blissful region beyond the seas.

The Papuans of New Guinea take pride in calling themselves the Coconut People. They hate the non-Papuans of their island who, they say, are not true Coconuts. They have a fantastic legend regarding the origin of the coconut. Even before the creation of man, their god killed another god, Somoali by name, who later became the god of the bushmen and the nomads. He placed the head of his victim on the bank of the Wamagao River, and after six nights, when he returned to see the head of his enemy, he found leaves sprouting from it. He then planted the sprouting head in the earth and from it grew the first coconut.

Most botanists seem to think that the original home of the coconut is not far from India, probably 'somewhere in the lands now under the sea, which existed in the western parts of the Indian Ocean'. All are agreed that its home is somewhere between Zanzibar and New Guinea. The seafaring Polynesians and wandering Malays probably carried it eastwards and westwards. It was probably the adventurous Polynesian mariners who first planted it in the New World.

The Malay seafarers, the once-maritime Tamils and the ancient mariners of the Bengal coast have probably been responsible for a much wider distribution of the coconut into the lands of the Indian Ocean. Ocean currents and monsoon drifts have also played a part in its spread.

So old is the plant in India that from early times the Arabs have called it the Indian Nut. Marco Polo called it by the same name. For Hindus it is the Kalpaka Vriksha, or Tree of Heaven.

Apart from the refreshing qualities of the flesh and water

of the coconut fruit, this tree has many uses. In Goa, brooms are made from the leaf ribs, while in Kerala the fermented sap is known as palm wine or toddy. The sugar from the sap gives us jaggery, the fibre from the outer rind provides coir fibre, the dry fleshy kernel provides copra and the oil extracted from the dry copra gives us coconut oil or coconut butter.

Several other palms are well-known in India—the tall, slim betel-nut palm; the shaggy wild date palm; and the palmyra palm, on whose strong leaves the ancient scriptures were written.

Trees of the Himalayas

Indwa is probably nowhere so rich in forests as in the Himalayas, where the hills and valleys provide so many contrasts in elevation, humidity and temperature that a great variety of vegetation is to be found all the year round.

Ascending the foothills, no very sudden change is noticed, and it almost seems that the vast stretch of forest lying in the still heat is merely a duplicate of the forest in the plains. But this is sal forest, which covers the foothills with speed and persistence. The more vigorous sal trees grow rapidly, the weaker bide their time until the death or destruction of their more powerful fellows.

A sal forest has a remarkably individual character, where, from tiny sapling to giant patriarch, each tree ruthlessly waits for the downfall of its neighbour: a restless, ambitious sea of foliage, some trees attaining a height of 150 feet and a girth of twenty feet.

The sal is the most important tree of the lower Himalayas, providing the bulk of railway sleepers in India and yielding, when tapped, a large quantity of good resin. The flowers, tiny and sweet-scented, appear in March, in some places heralding a spring festival, when baskets of them are carried from village to village and distributed to women as emblems of motherhood.

Beyond the sal forests, the hillside changes in appearance. The undergrowth is not so tall. It thins out, and the only features suggesting tropical vegetation are the giant mops of the screw pine and the beautiful tree ferns.

Now the birch and the poplar prevail. The Himalayan Birches, growing singly, are more valued for their bark than for their timber. The bark is cast off in wide, horizontal shreds, and is exported far and wide for tanning, papermaking and lining of hookahs. The poplar's broad, heart-shaped leaves readily flutter to every breeze; and apart from the tree's ornamental value, its close-grained timber is used for beams and rafters.

In the eastern hills, where the monsoon is heavy, the atmosphere is too humid for the coniferous family, but just suits the immigrant Japanese Cedar, which grows with such persistence that many of these trees, trim and beautiful and straight, are found at elevations of 4,000 to 6,000 feet— elevations which also happen to suit most of the flora of temperate Europe.

The oak and the chestnut grow profusely above 5,000 feet. The fruit of the chestnut is beloved by the Lepchas of Sikkim, and the wood of this tree provides the big pestles and mortars used for crashing millets, which are converted into local beer.

On the more exposed hills grow the maples, trees of no great size or thickness, but of striking appearance in the spring and autumn by the variety of crimson and gold tints in their foliage. There are several species of maple, and the best drinking cups in Tibet are made from the knobs of one particular kind of tree.

The walnut is a native of the eastern Himalayas, and bears a high percentage of good nuts. It is also in great demand for making furniture.

The rhododendrons and magnolias are the most admired trees of the Himalayas. The rhododendron's magnificent cluster of pink and crimson bells explains the meaning of its name—rhododendron, rose tree!

Near Darjeeling in West Bengal, the magnolia has deep wine-coloured flowers, which are very fragrant—so sweet that they have been known to cause giddiness to the inhaler.

The pine, deodar, cedar, yew and spruce are all well-known conifers in the Himalayas. Many beautiful bamboos abound in the hills—one species is used by the Lepchas for making bows, another is used in floating heavy logs and a third, when cut, shortened and flattened out, serves the purpose of tiles; it is durable and watertight.

The peach and the apricot, the plum and the cherry, grow wild and in cultivation, and their delicate pink and white blossoms add charm and grace to the grandeur of the Himalayas.

The Loveliness of Ferns

At the bottom of a hill there is a small rippling stream, its water almost hidden by the bright green tangled growth along its course. It is only by its sound, as it chatters over the pebbles, that we become aware of it. Here we come upon many plants that delight to grow in such a place—water mint, wild strawberries, wood sorrel, orchids and violets and dandelions, and a forest of ferns.

The first thing one notices is a beautiful group of ferns growing almost to the water. This is the lady fern, whose broad fronds must be almost four to five feet high—a delicate plant, frail and almost transparent in the fineness of its foliage, and looking so tender that you would think the sun and wind would almost scorch or shrivel it up; but the abundant supply of flowing water keeps these ferns cool and fresh. When the frosts of winter come, the fronds will crumple up into a heap of brown fragments, but their strength has by that time returned into the thick clump of root, to be stored and used for a still finer group of fronds next year.

In the moist parts of any forest there are sure to be several other kinds of fern, such as the male fern, with its strong upright fronds, looking just like a large green shuttlecock, three feet high. One of the commonest of Indian ferns is the maidenhair, which grows along the west coast and in the Himalayan foothills. During the monsoons it can be found on almost every wall and rock—a delicate, tender fern, easily torn by the wind.

On the stump of a fallen tree grow the prickly-toothed buckler fern and the broad buckler fern, whose rootlets penetrate the soft rotting wood to obtain their moisture. They are hardy, often remaining green throughout the winter. The handsome bracken fern often grow to a height of six or seven feet. Then there is the lovely hart's tongue fern, great clumps of which grow beside the forest path. It has broad green crinkled fronds and is quite unlike other ferns, but if you look at the back of the fronds you will see, from the little heap of rust-coloured spore-cases, that it is indeed a fern—all ferns grow their 'seeds' in this way.

There are several hundred varieties of fern. They are easily pressed and preserved. They may also be grown indoors in pots. But they are at their loveliest in the open, in cool damp places, in the depths of a forest or by the side of a mountain stream.

The history of ferns goes back into the mists of antiquity.

There was a time when they, and plants like them, filled the earth. It was a wet and dripping time. Flowers would have been of no use at all, but spores could carry on their life in the prevailing dampness. Some ferns grew as large as trees. The falling stems of these tree ferns were floated together by mighty streams, carried away to the sea and buried under sand and mud. The remains of these plants, being thus shut out from the air, could not rot but were slowly changed into coal. The impressions of the leaves and stems of these ferns can be distinguished even now, in many pieces of coal.

As the earth became drier, ferns retired to the shady and damp spots in which we now find them. They are a declining family, but let us hope they will remain with us for some time, for a forest stream without ferns would be like a maiden whose loveliest tresses have been shorn.

Cacti and Succulents

Half a dozen seedlings, very small and queerly shaped, make an instant appeal to would-be gardeners, especially young ones. The strange assortment of letters constituting their names are a challenge in themselves.

To their obvious appeal as small living things needing care, both cacti and succulents add the charm of continuing to live through a period of neglect. They survive knockings-over and being transplanted during enthusiastic periods, and though the very young plants do not flower, they very soon begin to grow 'young ones' in the oddest ways. The *bryophyllum tubiflorum*, for instance, which resembles a small rubbery Christmas tree, grows clusters of very tiny seedlings at the ends of its branches. Each of these have two leaves and a root, perfectly formed, and can be picked off with tweezers and planted in neat rows in a seed pan, where they soon grow into new trees.

Most succulents will grow a young plant on the broken

edge of a leaf, if the broken edge is inserted in suitable soil after being left to dry for a few days. The sempervivum family grow young ones all round, like chickens clustering round a hen, and *kleinia articulata* grows a new one on top of last year's old one. It will flower in winter, a fine cluster of leaves of bright green and tiny white flowers coming out of the topmost end of the bulb-like stem.

Most cacti are native to the warmer parts of the Americas, especially Mexico and the dry regions of South America. Some species grow in Africa; while others, such as the prickly pear and the night-flowering cactus, have long been naturalized in India. They are desert plants, and are able, by the peculiar structure of their leaves and stems, to endure long droughts.

The cactus family has more than a thousand members, all specially equipped to live in their surroundings. Unlike the leaves found in other plants, cactus plants have many sharp spines with little or no surface from which water could be lost by evaporation. A fleshy stem makes up the major part of the plant. These stems have vast water-storage spaces, which are filled whenever it rains. Many members of the cactus family are quite small, but some, such as the saguaro, reach up to seventy feet, often having as many as fifty branching arms.

Cacti and other succulents are not difficult to grow indoors, provided they can be given plenty of light and fresh air. They should be watered only moderately. Many people grow them for their fantastic shapes rather than for their individual blooms; but the plants must be seen in flower to be really appreciated. The prickly pear and the cereus have very showy flowers. The jumping cactus (so named not because it jumps, but because it will make you jump should you step on it) has beautiful white flowers, often larger than the parent plant. The Queen of the Night blooms only at night. The Christmas cactus bears lovely fuchsia-like blooms.

Cacti have their uses too. The roots of the yucca were used by the American Indians for soap, while in Mexico the prickly pear was cultivated because of the cochineal insect that lives on it and yields a red dye. In India, this cactus is generally used for hedges in gardens and fields.

The Jasmine

The jasmine has also been called the jessamine and jesse; its Arabic name is yasmin, and its Persian name jasemin. The white scented jasmine and the bright yellow winter jasmine (found mostly in the hills) are both native to India, and though they are cultivated in Western countries, they are essentially Eastern plants.

Various species of jasmine are grown in Indian gardens. The delicious fragrance of the flowers is particularly strong in the evening, for that is the time they open their blossoms—unlike most flowers, which open in the morning.

To obtain the evanescent odour of the flowers of the jasmine, a complicated process is necessary. To merely press them or distil them with water would be useless, the essence being too subtle to be captured by any such simple method.

The flowers must first be embedded in fat, to which they communicate their perfume, which is then separated from the fat and obtained in a more elegant form by means of alcohol. The last part of the process is quite modern, but the initial process is as old as the use of perfumes and explains the frequent use of ointments by people in ancient times.

The yellow winter jasmine is one of the prettiest wild flowers. It flowers in the hills in March and April, at a time when there are few other flowers in bloom. Its butter-yellow stars bring to life an otherwise drab hillside. The black shiny berries are eaten by blackbirds, bulbuls and other fruit-eating birds.

As the flowers appear when the plant is yet without a leaf, this hill species is sometimes called the naked jasmine. Such a plant is a pearl of great price, though it costs nothing and can be grown almost anywhere. The slender green angled stem will climb to a height of ten to twenty feet, and the branches, when in contact with the soil, will take root and form thickets of arching stems, soon covering a wide area.

The Flax

The flax, or linum, has been cultivated from before the Christian era, and over 500 years before the time of Homer, who speaks of it as representing an important domestic industry. In Switzerland its cultivation dates from the Stone Age.

Herodotus describes the Egyptian priests as wearing linen garments made from the fibre of the flax. In India, the plant has for long been cultivated not only for its fibres but also for the oil contained in its seeds, which we know of as linseed oil, or alsi-ki-tel.

The flax flower, which comes in both crimson and blue, will grow wild, or in a garden, or in a field. Though Oriental in origin, it is cultivated as far north as Norway. Its extremely light and airy style of growth makes it a most attractive plant.

The fibres inside the stem of the flax plant are very tough and can therefore be used for textile fabrics. To get the fibres, the plants are first stripped of their seeds and then steeped in water until partially rotten, when the gummy part of the stem is dissolved and the fibres loosened.

Next, to separate the woody portion of the stem, they are spread out to dry until the wood inside becomes brittle and breaks into pieces. The fibres are then drawn through a comb, called the 'hackle', where they are straightened out and freed from dust. The fibre thus gained has a fine, silky appearance, and is spun into yarn and finally woven into linen cloth.

The thread for making fine lace is usually spun in rooms kept almost dark, to discipline the eye and the fingers in the delicate task of rejecting all that is faulty, and obtaining a thread that is both fine and strong. It is said that the perfect thread should be as fine as the threads of a spider's web and as strong as a metal wire.

The Glory Lily

The *gloriosa superba*, or glory lily, is one of our most beautiful plants. During the rains it is often found shooting up in shady lanes or in bamboo thickets. The grace of its form, and the gaiety and warmth of its flowers, have resulted in the superb name the flower bears.

It is a fragile, weak climber, sprouting up from a tuberous root. Its round green stem is long and slender, and it has to seek the support of other plants and objects. For this purpose it uses its tapering tendril-like leaves. The plant climbs towards the freedom of the air and sunshine, unfurling its fire-flowers like triumphant banners. They have no scent, but the showy colours of their petals are able to attract insects.

The petals are at first bright yellow with scarlet tips, but as they grow older they become a dark crimson and bend further back. The insects find honey at the base of each petal, thrusting their tongues into the nectar while they hover in front of the flower.

The Water Lily

The beautiful lotus water lily is found in quiet waters everywhere—in peaceful lakes or tanks, and sometimes in artificial ponds. Not only is the lotus sacred to Hindus as the throne of the goddess Lakshmi, but the roots and seeds of a certain species are an edible and popular food.

The sacred lotus has large rose-coloured petals, but the more common water-lily has white sweet-scented flowers of a waxy appearance, which open in the morning and close later in the day. The flowers have many petals, arranged in rows, with stamens of a bright gold colour. It is a favourite subject with artists. The broad leaves spreading over the surface of the water like floating shields add a mysterious charm to a flower about which there are many myths and legends.

Most plants die if their roots and stems are kept under water, but the water lily has adapted itself to its surroundings.

The stem is thick and tuber-like, sending down long roots into the soft mud and preventing the plant from being carried away by the movement of water. The leaf stalks are long and reach to the surface, being attached to the centre of the leaf, which floats like a raft. The upper surface of the leaf is covered with a thin coat of wax, which prevents it from getting wet. Any water that touches it just rolls off as it would from a duck's back.

The flowers also float on the surface of the water at the end of long stalks. They open after sunrise, and are visited by insects that are attracted by the colour. But the insects only find pollen, as the plant does not secrete honey. Towards evening the flower closes again to protect itself from cold and damp.

When the small fruit of the water lily ripens and bursts, the seeds are carried wherever the water takes them until their protective bubble bursts. Then, being heavier than water, the seeds sink to the bottom and begin to form a new plant, often at some considerable distance from the old one.

Wild Flowers Near a Mountain Stream

Below my house is a forest of oak and maple and Himalayan rhododendron. A path twists its way down through the trees, over an open ridge where red sorrel grows wild, and then steeply down through a tangle of thorn bushes, vines and rangal bamboo. At the bottom of the hill the path leads on to a grassy verge, surrounded by wild rose. A stream runs close by the verge, tumbling over smooth pebbles, over rocks worn yellow with age, on its way to the plains and the little Song River and finally to the sacred Ganges.

When I first discovered the stream it was April and the wild roses were flowering, small white blossoms lying in clusters. There were primroses on the hill slopes, and an occasional late-flowering rhododendron provided a splash of red against the dark green of the hill.

The St John's Wort was flowering profusely on small shrubs.

Many legends have grown around this flower of pure dazzling sunshine which takes its family name—Hypericaceae—from the great Titan god Hyperion, who was the father of the Greek god of the sun, Apollo.

Is a friend of yours insane? Then get him to drink the sap from the leaves and stalks of the St John's Wort. He will be well again.

Are you hurt? If your wounds do not heal, take the juice and put it on the wound; and if the bleeding will not stop, take more juice.

Is your father bald? Then he must rise early one morning and bathe his head with the dew from St John's Wort, and his hair will grow again.

Do you live on the Isle of Man? Then beware! Tread not on the St John's Wort after sunset, lest a fairy horseman arise and carry you off. He will land you anywhere.

These are all English or Irish superstitions, but the St John's Wort is as profuse in the lower ranges of the Himalayas as it is anywhere in Europe.

A spotted forktail, a bird of the Himalayan streams, was much in evidence during those early visits. It moved nimbly over the boulders with a fairy tread, and continually wagged its tail.

In May and June, when the hills are always brown and dry, it remained cool and green near the stream, where ferns and maidenhair and long grasses continued to thrive. Downstream I found a cave with water dripping from the roof, the water spangled gold and silver in the shafts of sunlight that pushed through the slits in the cave roof. Few people came there. Sometimes a milkman or a coal-burner would cross the stream on his way to a village; but the nearby hill station's summer visitors had not discovered this haven of wild and green things.

The monkeys—langurs, with white and silver-grey fur, black faces and long swishing tails—had discovered the place, but they kept to the trees and sunlit slopes. They grew quite accustomed to my presence, and carried on with their work and play as though I did not exist. The young ones scuffled and wrestled like boys, while their parents attended to each other's toilets, stretching themselves out on the grass, beautiful animals with slim waists and long sinewy legs, and tails full of character. They were clean and polite, much nicer than the red monkeys of the plains.

During the rains the stream became a rushing torrent, bushes and small trees were swept away, and the friendly murmur of the water became a threatening boom. I did not visit the spot very often. There were leeches in the long grass, and they would fasten themselves on to my legs and feast on my blood. But it was always worthwhile tramping through the forest to feast my eyes on the foliage that sprang up in tropical profusion—soft, spongy moss; great stag ferns on the trunks of trees; mysterious and sometimes evil-looking orchids; the climbing convolvulus opening its purple secrets to the morning sun; and the wood sorrel, or oxalis—so named because of the oxalic acid derived from its roots—with its clover-like leaflets, which fold down like umbrellas at the first sign of rain.

And then, after a November hailstorm, it was winter, and one could not lie on the frostbitten grass. The sound of the stream was the same, but I missed the birds.

It snowed—the snow lay heavy on the branches of the oak trees and piled up in the culverts—and the grass and the ferns and wild flowers were pressed to sleep beneath a cold white blanket; but the stream flowed on, pushing its way through and under the whiteness, towards another river, towards another spring.

All Is Life

Whether by accident or design,
We are here.
Let's make the most of it, my friend.
Make happiness our pursuit,
Spread a little sunshine here and there.
Enjoy the flowers, the breeze,
Rivers, sea and sky,
Mountains and tall waving trees.
Greet the children passing by,
Talk to the old folk. Be kind, my friend.
Hold on, in times of pain and strife:
Until death comes, all is life.